IN A BLAZE OF POWER

JACK C. HARRIS
WRITER

JOE QUESADA
ART NICHOLS
PENCILLERS

ART NICHOLS
INKER

STEVE HAYNIE
LETTERER

CREATED ... QUESADA

THE RAY: IN A BLAZE OF POWER

Published by DC Comics. Cover and compilation copyright © 1994 DC Comics. All Rights Reserved.

Originally published in single magazine form as THE RAY 1-6. Copyright © 1991, 1992 DC Comics. All Rights Reserved. All characters, their distinctive likenesses and related indicia featured in this publication are trademarks of DC Comics. The stories, characters, and incidents featured in this publication are entirely fictional.

DC Comics, 1325 Avenue of the Americas, New York, NY 10019
A division of Warner Bros. — A Time Warner Entertainment Company
Printed in Canada. First Printing.
ISBN: 1-56389-090-9

Cover illustration by Joe Quesada and Brian Stelfreeze
Publication design by Brian Pearce

INTRODUCTION
BY ROBERT GREENBERGER

Who created The Ray?

The answer is sort of Will Eisner and mostly Lou Fine. You're scratching your heads and wondering who this Fine guy is, which mutant book did he draw and all that. Fuhgeddaboutit. Louis Kenneth Fine (1914-1971) is one of the most respected artists to work during the Golden Age of comics and he made The Ray a memorable character even though the character had a grand total of only 26 appearances for Quality Comics during that era. Quality Comics was the brainchild company of Everett "Busy" Arnold, one of the industry's pioneers. Quality was actually the number three top-selling company for a while (right behind DC and Archie), and they were also home to such classic creations as Plastic Man and the Blackhawks.

During the early 1940s, "Busy" Arnold paid top dollar for his talent and treated them well. He recognized Fine's exquisite art and hired him away from the famous Will Eisner/Jerry Iger studio. Fine was granted a private office all his own and was assigned feature after feature. These included sharing duties with the other top craftsman of that day, Reed Crandall, on such characters as Doll Man, Black Condor, Quicksilver, Uncle Sam, Neon the Unknown, Stormy Foster (don't ask) and finally, The Ray. When Fine and Crandall complained about fourth-rate stories, Arnold went out and hired the best writers he could find, and today those series hold up to rereading better than many of their contemporaries.

When SMASH COMICS needed a new feature, Eisner (who later entrusted The Spirit daily strip to Fine while he served in the armed forces during World War II) wrote and laid out the first Ray for Fine to complete. Fine went on to do about half of the 26 episodes that graced SMASH until it was replaced by a Spirit knock-off called Midnight. Fine left the business soon after for a successful career in commercial advertising and comic strips which lasted until his death in 1971.

The Ray's powers were never clearly defined although he stopped being human when an experimental balloon ride high into the atmosphere exposed him to harmful radiation (cosmic rays?— *nah*) and he became a coherent beam of light. He skipped around from having the ability to project light to being pure energy, to manipulating magnetism to riding light beams and the like. His strips allowed Fine (who often signed the feature E. Lectron) and Crandall and even Dave Berg (yes, Mad's "Lighter Side" guy) to display powerful yet graceful storytelling. Comics historian Jim Steranko has said, "If Crandall was a more realistic storyteller, Fine was more imaginative and stylized." Remember those last few words; we'll get back to them shortly.

DC purchased the Quality Comics' stable of super-heroes in 1956. They were resurrected from obscurity when writer Len Wein hit upon the idea of using them as catalysts for a Justice League of America summer crossover with the legendary Justice Society of America.

Later, in the short-lived FREEDOM FIGHTERS, The Ray was partnered with Black Condor (no, not the guy who had his own book last year), Firebrand (no, not the redhead from All-Star Squadron, but her brother), Phantom Lady (not the one from ACTION COMICS WEEKLY), Doll Man (not the one...never mind), the Human Bomb (a name with *hit* written all over it — not), and the spirit of America himself, Uncle Sam (yes, the one last seen in HAWK & DOVE #28). All of these characters were the mainstays of Quality Comics.

So much for the history lesson; on to Jim Owsley (editor) and Jack C. Harris (writer) and their interpretation of The Ray.

Lou Fine's work has been cited by both Harris and Owsley as initially attracting them to The Ray. Jack says he recalls being floored by Fine's artwork in one of the earliest comics he ever read. Jim recalls being thoroughly impressed when Archie Goodwin saw fit to reprint one of those stories back when DETECTIVE COMICS was a 100-pager (and for 50¢ no less).

While both men were inspired by Fine's incredibly graceful work, they needed someone with an "imaginative and stylized" technique to bring the ideas to life. Fortunately, Owz had begun working with a newcomer named Joe Quesada on TSR's FORGOTTEN REALMS. Joe gave them everything they asked for and more. With a quirky storyline, an inspired take on the character (including a link between the new Ray with the old work that wasn't clichéd), and raw energy in the art, this mini-series became a sleeper hit. THE RAY propelled Jack back into comics on a more or less full-time basis, it made a megastar out of Joe Quesada, and it even made people sit up and pay attention to Jim's other work at DC which included another Quality revival, the Black Condor, simultaneously re-created entirely by Brian Augustyn.

Why has it taken DC this long to get The Ray back into print?

Actually, a whole host of factors meant this series would be launched after many fits and starts. The good news is that Owz, who originally edited *Spider-Man* for Marvel and then wrote it, repeats the formula by first editing THE RAY and now writing it, this time for Mr. Brian Augustyn. With Joe Quesada booked until the next millennium, Mr. A cast about and helped discover Howard Porter, a quiet young man not unlike Ray Terrill, although Howard doesn't glow at night...as far as we know. Inking comes from Robert Jones, a young man whose talent has grown with each passing year.

Rounding out the new creative team, we'll have ace letterer Ken Bruzenak and colorist Pat Garrahy (yeah, okay, the first one's by Gloria Vasquez but she got overcommitted and had to give it up).

What may confuse you all is the advertising announcing the writer as Christopher Priest. It's okay, it's really Owz. The reasons behind the official and legally binding name change are left for greater minds than mine to fathom. Personally, I think it's all a legal clerk's fault — he misread Jim's handwritten form asking for the recently vacated name Prince and was assigned Priest. The Christopher was an afterthought. We're now asked to call Owz Priest, but I think I'm just going to call him Father.

That's the whole sordid tale. Now go ahead and enjoy this story which remains certainly worthy of rereading and is kind of a tribute to the amazing work of Lou Fine which brought both Jack and JimOwzPriest together to make magic.

Robert Greenberger, Manager-Editorial Scheduling, has been a part of DC Comics for the last decade. In addition to making up deadlines, he knows far too much of the company's history for his own good although it meant he was qualified to write this introduction.

IMPRESSIVE, COUSIN. HOW DID IT *FEEL?*

THAT... THAT WAS *INCREDIBLE...* LIKE TASTING FOOD FOR THE FIRST TIME...

...AFTER *STARVING* ALL YOUR LIFE...

SO, YOU *MUST* BE CONVINCED THAT YOU'VE INHERITED YOUR OLD MAN'S POWERS NOW, RIGHT?

YEAH...YEAH, THAT'S THE ONLY *EXPLANATION* FOR WHAT JUST HAPPENED TO ME...

NOW YOU KNOW THE *REAL* REASON HE KEPT YOU OUT OF *SUNLIGHT* ALL YOUR LIFE.

YO, RAY-- YOU CAN DO JUST ABOUT *ANYTHING!* YOU'RE GOING TO MAKE SOME KINDA *HERO!*

NO. UH-UH! NO WAY! *THE RAY* IS DEAD AND BURIED AND ALMOST *FORGOTTEN.* HE'S GOING TO *STAY* THAT WAY!

"YOU'RE ONLY MY *COUSIN,* HANK. YOU DIDN'T *LIVE* WITH HIM ALL THESE YEARS. REMEMBER, MY DAD *HID* THESE POWERS FROM ME ALL MY LIFE! HE DIDN'T *WANT* ME TO BE A HERO!"

H. TERRILL 1921 - 1992

"I THINK YOU'RE *WRONG,* RAY, BUT WHO KNOWS, YOU MIGHT EVENTUALLY SEE THE *LIGHT...*"

ELSEWHERE...

CHICKFFFFWWOOSSSH!

8

AND I GOT SOME *GAMES* AND SOME, YOU KNOW, *CLOTHES* AND LOOKIT *THIS--* SUPER FRIENDS ACTION FIGURES!

WE'RE SPEAKING WITH *RAYMOND TERRILL,* THE CELEBRATED *NIGHT BOY,* ON THE OCCASION OF HIS *EIGHTH* BIRTHDAY...

TELL ME, RAYMOND ...I...

...PARTY FOR *ME!*

ZOOM! HERE THEY GO!

WELL, MR. TERRILL, HE SEEMS PERFECTLY *NORMAL* TO ME...

...ALTHOUGH IT'S A LITTLE TOUGH TO *TAPE* FOR BROADCAST...

"YEAH, IT ALL *SEEMED* NORMAL TO *ME* BACK THEN. I THOUGHT *EVERYBODY* HAD BIRTHDAYS IN THE MIDDLE OF THE *NIGHT...*"

HA! WELL, HE'S *ALL BOY...*

TELL OUR *LISTENERS,* MR. TERRILL, HOW *LONG* MUST HE TOTALLY *SHUN* THE DAYLIGHT?

ALL HIS *LIFE,* MR. KOLPAN. THANKFULLY, HE'S *ADJUSTED* EXCEPTIONALLY WELL.

AND WHAT ABOUT HIS *SCHOOLING?* HE *CAN'T* ATTEND REGULAR CLASSES...

OF *COURSE* NOT. HE HAS A PAIR OF WONDERFUL *PRIVATE TUTORS...*

IT'S *READY,* SISTER...

HUMMPH...

SO TH' *ROCKET MAN FALLS...!*

HAPPY BIRTHDAY, RAYMOND!

KLAK KLAK KLAK

HI, JENNY!

"MOST NIGHTS I PLAYED WITH MY NEIGHBOR, JENNY JURDEN..."

SURE. ROCKET MAN'S ALL *BETTER* NOW.

CAN I PLAY?

YOU CAN HAVE HIM SINCE YOU'RE MY *BESTUS* FRIEND.

I *AM?* THEN HOLD OUT YOUR HAND...

THIS IS FOR YOU... MY MAGIC CIRCUS LIGHT...

FOR *KEEPS?* IS IT *REAL* MAGIC?

HALY CIRCUS

COME, CHILDREN! TIME FOR CAKE!

HUMMPH...

HAPPY BIRTHDAY TO YOU, HAPPY BIRTHDAY TO YOU, HAPPY BIRTHDAY, DEAR RAYMOND...

"YEAH... WE PLAYED TOGETHER UNTIL THE NIGHT OF MY *EIGHTH* BIRTHDAY..."

PPFFOOOPHH

"SOMETHING *HAPPENED* THAT NIGHT... I CAN'T REMEMBER JUST WHAT IT WAS..."

OH, MY...

...GRACIOUS!

TIME TO GO HOME, HONEY!

MOMMY! THE PARTY'S NOT *OVER!*

JENNY! DON'T GO!

"I DIDN'T SEE MUCH OF HER *AFTER* THAT. MOST PEOPLE STAYED *AWAY* FROM MY HOUSE. WITH ITS *PAINTED-OVER WINDOWS* I GUESS IT LOOKED PRETTY *SPOOKY*."

"BUT SHE *REMEMBERED* ME THROUGH THE YEARS-- EVEN WHEN HER FRIENDS *RODE* HER ABOUT KNOWING ME..."

"THAT'S WHAT I *LEARNED* AFTER SHE *CALLED ME* THAT DAY..."

BON JOVI
IN CONCERT
THE SPECTRUM

RAY! TELEPHONE!

"IT WAS *JEN!* SHE WAS INVITING ME TO THE *JUNIOR PROM!*"

BOOM

WHO'S THE *GEEK* IN THE HAT AND SHADES?

THAT'S *NIGHT BOY!* HE CAN'T TAKE THE LIGHTS! HA!

I REALLY *APPRECIATE* YOU INVITING ME, JENNIFER.

I JUST WISH I COULD HAVE GONE OUT AND BOUGHT *YOU* SOMETHING...

OH, RAY, DON'T BE *SILLY*.

I JUST WANTED YOU TO HAVE SOME *FUN*...

AFTER ALL, I'M *STILL* YOUR "BESTUS" FRIEND!

HUH! *BEST* FRIEND... MORE LIKE *ONLY* FRIEND!

THAT WAS THE LAST TIME I *SAW* HER.

LOOK AT IT THIS WAY, DUDE --SHE'S PROBABLY FORGOTTEN YOU BY NOW.

AFTER ALL --YOU'RE *BORING*.

I'M JUST NOT IN THE *MOOD.*

GIVE ME A *BREAK,* HANK.

I WAS FINALLY GETTING *USED* TO EVERYTHING. I CAN HACK WITH THE *BEST* OF THEM ON MY COMPUTER...

...PULL IN DATA FROM *EVERYWHERE* ...I COULD EVEN MAKE A *LIVING* WORKING FROM HOME...

WAKE ME WHEN YOU'RE DONE FEELING SORRY FOR YOURSELF, OKAY?

SORRY IF ALL THIS TRAGEDY IN MY LIFE DEPRESSES YOU, HANK--

--I GUESS YOU'VE NEVER HAD TO WATCH YOUR FATHER DIE...

DAD? DID YOU *CALL* ME, DAD?

YES... SON... COME IN. CLOSE THE DOOR...

L...LOOK THERE...

YOUR *DESK?* YOU SAID NEVER TO TOUCH IT...

TOUCH IT NOW... OPEN IT... READ THE ALBUM...

QUIT... DIDN'T WANT THE *BURDEN*... WANTED A *NORMAL* LIFE... A *FAMILY*...

THE BANNER

THE RAY QUITS!

...Y SUPER-HERO VANISHES FROM SIGHT
...M FIGHTERS VOW TO CARRY ON

"MET... YOUR MOTHER... MARRIED... MOVED OUT WEST.

"EVERYTHING WAS GOOD... WORKING... WRITING... YOU WERE ON THE WAY.

"THEN THE NIGHT YOU WERE *BORN*... CALLED TO THE *EMERGENCY* ROOM."

EMERGENCY

AMBULANCE

EMERGENCY WARD

DOCTOR! MY *WIFE*--?!

SHE'S PERFECTLY *FINE*, MR. TERRILL. IT'S YOUR *SON* THAT CONCERNS ME.

M-MY *SON?* IT'S A BOY?

WELL, I *THINK* SO. IT'S JUST THAT WE HAVEN'T BEEN ABLE TO GET *CLOSE* ENOUGH FOR A THOROUGH EXAMINATION!

BY ALL THAT'S HOLY! HIS... HIS *ENERGY* OUTPUT. HE'S *INHERITED* MY POWERS. BUT HOW? AN *ACQUIRED* TRAIT CAN'T BE INHERITED!

DOCTOR! TURN OUT THE *LIGHTS!*

9

TERRILL! DON'T GO IN THERE--

I said "TURN OUT THE LIGHTS!"

SPATZZZ SPATZZZ

THERE, THERE, BE QUIET, SPORT.

YOU SEE, I CAN ABSORB YOUR ENERGY.

AND WITHOUT LIGHTS, YOU CAN'T RECHARGE.

IT'S SAFE NOW, DOCTOR. YOU CAN COME IN.

WH-WHAT'S THIS ALL ABOUT?

DOCTOR, HAVE YOU EVER HEARD OF... THE RAY?

CLACK!

"TOLD HIM... EVERYTHING... AND THEN HE HAD A THEORY..."

THOSE POWERS OF YOURS...

...THEY MUST HAVE ALTERED YOUR GENETIC MAKEUP, YOUR DNA...

THEN THAT'S HOW HE INHERITED MY POWERS...

BUT HOW CAN AN INFANT CONTROL SUCH POWER?

THAT'S JUST THE PROBLEM... HE CAN'T!

THAT'S WHEN THE DOCTOR SUGGESTED THE... THE LIE... TO TELL EVERYONE... INCLUDING YOUR MOTHER...

...THAT YOU WERE ALLERGIC TO SUNLIGHT ...THAT EXPOSURE WOULD BE FATAL... THAT YOU HAD ...TO LIVE IN THE DARK.

FORGIVE US, RAY, FORGIVE US...

10

"THEN HE WAS *GONE*.

"THE REALIZATION THAT I COULD LIVE IN THE *SUN* WAS *LOST* ON ME. I SCHEDULED AT *NIGHT* OUT OF *HABIT*...

"I HARDLY REMEMBER HIS *FUNERAL*, BUT THINKING *BACK* I REALIZE THAT SOME OF THE PEOPLE THERE MUST HAVE BEEN *OTHER* SUPER-HEROES IN THEIR *REAL* IDENTITIES.

"I WOULD HAVE SPENT THE REST OF THE NIGHT IN THE *MEN'S ROOM* IF IT HADN'T BEEN FOR *YOU*."

GENTLEMEN

HEY! HOLD DOWN THAT RACKET, WILLYA?

THE *HEAD* IS A SACRED PLACE OF SOLITUDE, G! A SHRINE MEANT FOR QUIET REFLECTION...

YOU WERE SMOKING A CIGARETTE.

YEAH, BUT IT'S A GREAT SPEECH.

JUST WHO THE HECK ARE *YOU*?

OH, SORRY. I'M *HANK* TERRILL. I THINK WE'RE *COUSINS*.

ALL THAT SECOND-COUSIN-TWICE-REMOVED STUFF HAS ALWAYS CONFUSED ME, BUT WE *ARE* RELATED. I'VE COME TO PAY MY SIDE OF THE FAMILY'S *RESPECTS*.

OH, WELL, UH, THANKS.

WE'D BETTER GET BACK IN THERE.

WAIT UP, G. SOMETHING I GOTTA *WARN* YOU ABOUT...

THIS'LL BE *GREAT!* SHE'LL BE *FLOORED* TO SEE ME IN THE *DAYTIME.*

MAYBE SHE'S FREE FOR *LUNCH.* WE CAN TALK LIKE WE *USED* TO. WE CAN...

WE'RE *HERE,* KID.

HUH? *ALREADY?*

AMAZING, AIN'T IT? FIVE-FIFTY, KID.

TAXI

THERE IT IS. I GUESS I'LL HAVE TO GO ASK SOMEONE WHICH *OFFICE* SHE WORKS IN...

24 HOUR TELLER

FIRST FEDERAL SAVINGS OF PHILADELPHIA

I--*KRIPES!* THERE SHE IS! RIGHT IN FRONT OF THE *WINDOW!*

MAN! I SHOULD HAVE *CALLED* FIRST. WHAT AM I GOING TO *SAY* TO HER?

MAYBE SHE WAS JUST BEING *NICE* TO THE LITTLE *HANDICAPPED BOY* NEXT DOOR BACK THEN...

SHE'S JUST--*HEY!* WHAT THE--?

STRUGGLE AND I PULL THE *TRIGGER!*

UMMPH--!

14

24

25

NO WIFE OF *MINE* IS GOING TO GET *BURNED UP* BY SOME SUPER *FREAK!*

WIFE? HE... HE SAID *WIFE!* UNN...

Y-YES, DEAR... BUT *SOMEONE'S* GOT TO HELP HIM...

OOO... WH-WHAT *HAPPENED?* EVERYTHING WENT *FUZZY...*

GRACIOUS!

PRETTY *DARING...* EVEN FOR A *HERO!*

MEOW?

OH *KRIPES!* I BURNED OFF MY *PANTS!*

I'VE GOT TO GET *OUT OF HERE!*

WHAT'S EVERYONE *STARING* AT? I'VE *STOPPED* GLOWING! AND...

HA! HA! SO, HE TAKES HIS FIRST *TRUE STEPS* IN *BARE FEET!* ALL IS *WELL...*

26

SOON, BACK AT RAY'S MOTEL...

COUSIN HANK WAS *RIGHT!* I *COULD* BE A SUPER-HERO IF I *WANTED*...

BUT WHAT'S THE *USE?* I DIDN'T EVEN GET THE *GIRL* IN THE END!

MARRIED... JENNIFER'S *MARRIED*...

I GUESS I DON'T HAVE TO KEEP HER CIRCUS *FLASHLIGHT* ANY LONGER...

WHAT'S *THIS*...?

HUMMPH! I DIDN'T EVEN KNOW I WAS STILL *CARRYING* THIS!

I...I GUESS I'LL TOSS *IT* TOO...

HMMM... THE *LIGHT* IS WHAT DOES IT... I CAN *FEEL* IT...

UNNNN...

HUH? THE BATTERY'S BEEN DEAD IN THIS THING FOR YEARS--

--AND IT PRACTICALLY *BLINDS* ME?!

SAVE ME!

HUH? WHAT--?

SAVE *ME*, RAY!

IT'S...COMING FROM THE BATHROOM--!

27

28

THAT OLD HOUSE

RAY TERRILL WAS RAISED IN THE *DARK,* TOLD HE WAS *ALLERGIC* TO THE *LIGHT.*

THIS WAS A *LIE.*

RAY TERRILL WAS TOLD THAT HE WOULD *DIE* IF HE WAS EVER EXPOSED TO *SUNLIGHT.*

THIS, TOO, WAS A *LIE.*

RAY TERRILL LEARNED THAT HIS LATE *FATHER* WAS REALLY THE 1940'S *SUPER-HERO* -- *THE RAY* -- AND THAT HE'D *INHERITED* HIS SUPER POWERS.

NOW, FACE TO FACE WITH A *GLOWING,* STRANGELY GARBED FIGURE IN HIS MOTEL *BATHROOM,* RAY TERRILL WONDERS IF THAT *TOO* WAS A LIE!

WHO... ARE YOU?

I *TOLD* YOU! I'M *THE RAY!*

YOU *CAN'T* BE! MY *FATHER* WAS THE RAY... AND HE'S *DEAD!*

...I'M TELLING ...THE *TRUTH.* I'VE COME FOR YOUR HELP...

spatz

spatz

S-STAY BACK.

YOU'VE GOT TO *HELP* ME, SON... BUT OUR POWERS *NEUTRALIZE* EACH OTHER WHEN WE'RE IN PROXIMITY...

YOU *CAN'T...*

YOU'VE GOT TO *HELLLLL...*⚡

POOM

HEY!

228

FWIZZZZZZZZZ

WHY THE HECK AM I *SURPRISED?* NOTHING IN THE PAST *48 HOURS* HAS GONE LIKE I'VE EXPECTED! I...

WAIT A MINUTE! WHOEVER THAT GUY WAS-- I'VE GOT TO *CATCH* HIM--

HE'S GOT SOME *ANSWERS!*

SIN

ICE

2

I'M

GOING

TOO

FAST

PHILADELPHIA'S FAMOUS ITALIAN MARKET...

FERRARA'S
FISH·MARKET
FRESH DAILY

LOWEST PRICES TOWN

PALMOTTI'S POULTRY

AAF
POULT
EGGS

TO

STOP

MYSELF!

WHUMF

JEAN
½ OFF

OWCH!

FLY
YOU
BUT

½ OFF
ALL

ALL T-S
½ PR

WOOO.
I THINK
I HURT MY
NECK...

GOT TO
DRAW IN THIS
HEAT OR I'LL
BLISTER THE
PAINT ON
THIS CAR.

BRR!
TURNING OFF
THE HEAT SUDDENLY
LIKE THAT MAKES
IT...

...COLD...?

MAMA MIA!
NUDO UOMO!

TITO & MARIA'S BAKE

RUBINSTEIN'S
KOSHER
ITALIAN
SAUSAGE

33

34

THIS IS YOUR STOP, KID. HEE HEE HEE MMMEFF HAHA

BUS STOP

THANKS... I SUPPOSE IT WOULD'VE BEEN TOO MUCH EFFORT FOR THAT GIRL TO FIND SOMETHING IN MY SIZE...

SHOULD'VE GONE BACK TO THE MOTEL... BUT HOME WAS CLOSER. HOPEFULLY THERE WON'T BE ANY--

--REPORTERS HANGING AROUND--

VROOOM

EXCUSE ME! EXCUSE ME! YOU'RE RAYMOND TERRILL, RIGHT? I'M NICK BILLINGS OF THE PHILADELPHIA DAILY BULLETIN. CAN WE TALK A MOMENT?

YES, YES. I WANT TO TALK ABOUT YOUR AMAZING CURE!

CURE?

YES! DIDN'T YOU USED TO BE THE NIGHT BOY-- CONDEMNED TO LIVE IN THE DARK?

NOW HERE YOU ARE BASKING IN THE SUN! HOW--

SORRY, CALL ME SOME OTHER TIME!

HE'S THE REASON I WAS HOLED UP IN THAT MOTEL. I DON'T NEED SOMEONE DIGGING THROUGH MY LIFE WHEN EVEN I HAVEN'T EVEN SHOVELED DEEP ENOUGH MYSELF!

NIGHT BOY.

I GOTTA GET A LIFE...

SLAM

UPSTAIRS...

ONLY THING OF MINE LEFT HERE WAS THIS OLD JACKET!

KRIPES... ALL DAD'S CLOTHES ARE PACKED AWAY! LOOKS LIKE I'M STUCK WITH THESE DUDS...HEY... LOOSE PAGES FROM DAD'S SCRAPBOOK...

PROPERTY OF RONOR CLASS

HEY... WEIRD... THESE PHOTOS OF THE RAY... THEY... THEY DON'T LOOK LIKE DAD, REALLY. THEY LOOK LIKE THAT GUY IN THE... MOTEL... HOW COULD...?

CLICK!

YIKE! THAT'S THE FRONT DOOR. DID THAT REPORTER JUST WALK RIGHT IN?

7

NO...IT'S MY DAD'S LAWYER--

HI, MR. BRETT.

OH, *RAYMOND.* EXCUSE ME. I DIDN'T REALIZE YOU'D *RETURNED.* I USED MY OWN KEY...

WELL, I'M GLAD I'VE *FOUND* YOU HERE. THERE ARE A NUMBER OF *DOCUMENTS* YOU NEED TO SIGN...

AS YOUR FATHER'S *SOLE HEIR,* YOU NEED TO TRANSFER *POWER OF ATTORNEY* TO *ME* SO WE CAN PUT THE HOUSE ON THE *MARKET.*

THE *HOUSE* ON THE *MARKET?* SELL MY *HOUSE?* I HAVE TO *SELL* MY HOUSE?

OF *COURSE.* HOW ELSE CAN YOU PAY THE OUTSTANDING *LEGAL FEES* YOUR FATHER'S ESTATE OWES?

C-CAN'T I READ THIS JUNK ALL *OVER*...YOU KNOW, AND SIGN IT *TOMORROW?*

SORRY. THIS HAS TO BE COMPLETED BY THE END OF *BUSINESS HOURS TODAY*...

OKAY... OKAY...

HMMMM...THAT'S *NATHANIEL BRETT,* THE *LAWYER*... MAYBE I CAN DIG THROUGH THE PAPER'S FILES ON *HIM!*

ROT!

SELLING THE HOUSE? BUT--BUT--

--I LIVE HERE--

ELSEWHERE...

HMMMM... UNFAVORABLE EMOTIONS AND *ANXIETY* FROM THE BOY ONLY *HAMPER* HIS MELIORATION... AND THE DANGER DRAWS *CLOSER* EVER STILL! AH, *WOE* UPON THE WORLD...

8

36

HERE IT IS... PRETTY CLEAR, EH?

TAP TAP

1:30 PM

YES, BUT CAN YOU *REWIND IT* BACK A FEW SECONDS...

SURE THING, *MS. JURDEN.*

WHIRWHIRWHIRWHIR click

UH--? THAT'S *IMPOSSIBLE!*

EXCUSE ME?

THANK YOU.

HEY, *JENNIFER!* WHAT'S *WRONG?*

LAY *OFF*, CLIFF. 24 *HOURS* AGO SHE WAS A *HOSTAGE* IN A BANK HEIST. WATCHIN' THE SECURITY TAPE IS *BOUND* TA SHAKE 'ER UP!

1:30 PM

PAUSE

HMMM. HE *SPOOKED* HER ...SHE *SAW* HIM BEFORE HE *CHANGED...* UNFORTUNATE...

IT *WAS!* IT WAS *RAY TERRILL* OUTSIDE THE BANK.

BUT *HOW?* HOW COULD HE BE *OUT* IN THE *MIDDLE OF THE DAY?* THE SUNLIGHT WOULD HAVE *KILLED* HIM!

I'VE GOT TO BE BY *MYSELF*... SORT IT OUT...

THERE! IT IS SHE!

TELLER

FIRST FEDERAL SAVINGS

IT'S NOT FAIR. IT'S *NOT.*

I *LIVE* HERE! I--

RAYMOND ...HELP ...ME

YIKES! WHAT DO Y--!?

GONE? OR WAS HE *THERE* AT ALL?

FLY YOUR BUTTON

SOMEONE'S AT THE *DOOR*--

RING RING RING

RAYMOND... HELP... ME

GONE SWEET HOME

...NUTS...

RING RING RING

RING RING

YOU!

WHATUP, G?

NICE OUTFIT.

--WHAT THE FREAK IS GOING **ON**, HANK?!?

WELL, AT THE MOMENT, YOU'RE STRETCHIN' OUT MY LEATHER.

IN A MINUTE, I'M GONNA SMACK THE SPIT OUT OF YOU.

SORRY. SORRY. I'VE BEEN SEEING SOME REALLY **WEIRD** THINGS SINCE YOU LEFT.

WEIRD THINGS...?

YEAH. I KEEP SEEING SOME GUY DRESSED UP LIKE *THE RAY* CALLING FOR **HELP**! IT'S **NUTS**!

MAYBE IT'S THESE **DIGS**, G. YOU OUGHT TO **DITCH** THEM. YOU KNOW, GRAB THE CASH AND GET YOURSELF A **RAD PAD** SOMEWHERE DOWNTOWN...

...LIKE SOUTH STREET --NEAR THE PHOENIX... FLY HONIES TEN DEEP--

YOU SOUND LIKE DAD'S **LAWYER**! I DON'T **WANT** TO SELL THIS HOUSE. KRIPES, THIS IS MY WHOLE **WORLD**!

I'VE SPENT 90% OF MY **LIFE** IN THIS HOUSE! I **CAN'T** CHUCK IT ALL **OVERNIGHT**! I **CAN'T**! YOU SEE THAT, DON'T YOU--?

GLAD TO KNOW YOU'RE THERE FOR ME, HANK.

YO, I'M YOUR **COUSIN**, G.

YOU WANT A **KEY**, DON'T YOU.

SEVERAL.

LOOK, HANK I'M **NOT** LIKE EVERYONE ELSE...

...JUST LIKE YOU'VE BEEN **TELLING** ME!

BUT YOU'LL **GET** YOUR WAY. THE HOUSE **IS** FOR SALE. I'M MOVING **OUT**, BUT I DON'T KNOW WHERE **TO**. MAYBE I'LL--

RING RING RING

THE DOOR BELL...

OH, **NO**, NOT **AGAIN!** IT'S PROBABLY THAT **REPORTER** OR **BRETT** OR WHO KNOWS, MAYBE IT'S AN **I.R.S.** AGENT.

YOU ANSWER IT! TELL 'EM I'VE **MOVED OUT!** TELL 'EM I'M **DEAD!**

HMMM...

RING RING

WELL! WELL! HUHH--LOWW, RADIANCE!

UMMM... DOES...DOES **RAY TERRILL** STILL LIVE HERE?

I WONDER HOW MANY MORE OF THESE **SCRAPBOOK** PAGES ARE TUCKED AWAY IN THIS HOUSE...

RAY SAVES ALLIAN

THAT **DOES** IT! I **CAN'T** SELL THIS PLACE UNTIL I CAN DIG OUT MORE **ANSWERS** FROM IT!

I'M CALLING **BRETT** AND RENEGING ON THAT **POWER** OF ATTORNEY DEAL!

RAAAAYMOND!

YIKES!

YO, *RAY!* YOU GOT SOME *COMPANY!*

OKAY, *GHOST*, OR *SPIRIT* OR *FIGMENT* OF MY IMAGINATION --WE'RE GOING TO HAVE A *SHOWDOWN!*

YOU DON'T KNOW THE *HALF* OF IT, HANK!

I...I'M *JENNIFER JURDEN.* I'M A *FRIEND* OF RAY TERRILL'S...

YEAH, YEAH. I'M HIS *COUSIN HANK.* RAY'S *DEAD.*

THEN WHY WERE YOU *CALLING UPSTAIRS* --?

ALL RIGHT, I'M *STUMPED.*

RAY...?

NO ONE HERE... HE COULDN'T HAVE FLOWN OUT THE WINDOW...

COULD HE...?

ELSEWHERE...

AH, PERHAPS NOW HE SHALL *ESCAPE* ENTANGLEMENTS AND BE *FREE* TO MEET HIS DESTINY.

ALL ARE IN POSITION...THE AFFAIR CRIES *HASTE* AND *SPEED* MUST ANSWER IT...

41

43

WAS NOCH DAS?

OW!

OW!

OW!

OW!

ROT!

SPLOSHHHH

BLICK! UM FALLEN AUS *FLUGPLATZ!*

OW! I THINK I HURT MY *NECK* AGAIN!

HEY! WHY'S IT SO *DARK?*

OH! *HI.* LOOK, CAN YOU TELL ME WHAT PART OF TOWN I'M--I *UMM...*

ZUDECKEN!

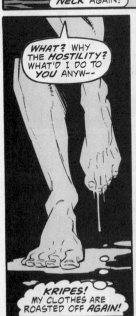

WHAT? WHY THE *HOSTILITY? WHAT'D* I DO TO *YOU* ANYW--

KRIPES! MY CLOTHES ARE ROASTED OFF *AGAIN!*

UMMM...HEH... WELL, I CAN EXPLAIN.

DU VERDUBEN!

FOP

THE HEIDELBERG PRISON, SOME HOURS LATER...

ACH, FRISCH FISCH!

I WANT TO GO HOME.

I WANT TO GO HOME NOW.

KRIPES, HOW FAST WAS I TRAVELING? ONE SECOND I'M OVER PHILADELPHIA AND THE NEXT THING I KNOW I'M IN GERMANY, I THINK.

MY POWER... IS GONE! IT'S LIKE I BURNED IT ALL UP OR SOMETHING--

...I COULD BE STUCK HERE... FOREVER.

HEY! HOLD ON! DON'T I GET A PHONE CALL!

HEZ, AMERIKANISH, ICH GESACHT JACKE!

TEL-E-PHONE?

DOES ANYONE SPEAK ENGLISH?

HOME...

...I DON'T EVEN *HAVE* A HOME ANYMORE! AND NOW THAT I'VE BURNED OUT THOSE FREAKY *POWERS*...

...I'D HAVE NO WAY OF GETTING THERE!

STRANDED... THOUSANDS OF MILES AWAY... IN A CELL BLOCK FILLED WITH DRUNKS...GOT TO FACE IT...

...AS AN ADULT, I'M A TOTAL WASHOUT--

RAYMOND...

49

THE PHILADELPHIA OFFICES OF BRETT, RICH, LIVINGSTON & STEEN...

COLLECT CALL FROM RAY TERRILL, MR. BRETT.

I'VE GOT IT, MS. JOVANOVICH...

YES, RAYMOND?

MR. BRETT... I JUST WANTED TO CALL YOU AND TELL YOU THAT THERE WON'T BE ANY PROBLEMS ABOUT VACATING THE HOUSE AS SOON AS POSSIBLE.

I'LL BE LOOKING FOR AN APARTMENT SOON.

OKAY, RAYMOND... THANK YOU...

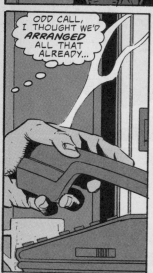

ODD CALL, I THOUGHT WE'D ARRANGED ALL THAT ALREADY...

MR. BRETT, WHY'D YOU ACCEPT A COLLECT CALL ALL THE WAY FROM GERMANY?

GERMANY?!

GO FIGURE! COME 6 A.M. AND THEY RELEASED ALL THE NIGHTLY PERVERTS... INCLUDING ME.

CALLED TO HIT BRETT UP FOR A PLANE TICKET...

...BUT I HAVEN'T FIGURED OUT HOW TO EXPLAIN ALL THIS!

SO, LOOKS LIKE I'M STUCK.

JUST AS WELL. DAD'S DEAD... JENNY'S MARRIED... HANK'S JUST TOO WEIRD...

MEOW?

AT LEAST THE SUN'S COMING UP. MAYBE I'M BECOMING A MORNING PERSON AFTER ALL THESE YEARS...

ELSEWHERE...

AHH! HE IS COMPLACENT! IF HE ACCEPTS HIS ROLE, WELL AND GOOD. BUT HIS TRAINING MUST BE COMPLETED! THE DANGER GROWS NEARER AND THE TIME GROWS SHORT!

NEXT:

RAY SETTLES DOWN IN BERLIN WITH A CHEESEMAKER'S DAUGHTER AND TAKES A JOB PRESSING PORSCHE HUBCAPS! THAT, OR HE BATTLES AN ERUPTING VOLCANO -- YOU DECIDE!!

BY THE WAY, WHO IS THIS GEEK, ANYWAY?!

50

4,525 MILES *EAST* OF PHILADELPHIA...

MMMM? OWW! MY *NECK*...

--MAN! WHAT A *FREAKY DREAM*--

I DREAMED I ZAPPED MYSELF TO GERMANY FAST ENOUGH TO BURN MY *CLOTHES* OFF AND GOT ARRESTED AS A *PERVERT!*

IT *WAS* A *DREAM,* RIGHT--?

...LIKE I'M WAITING FOR THE CAT TO TELL ME...

I HAVE ABSOLUTELY NO APPRECIATION OF THE IRONY IN ALL THIS.

WELL, WHAT *NOW?*

THERE'S NO SIGN OF THAT DIP IN THE YELLOW TIGHTS CLAIMING TO BE *THE RAY.* NOT THAT HE'D BE OF ANY HELP *ANYWAY.*

I CHOKED WHEN I CALLED BRETT FOR A PLANE TICKET-- COULDN'T THINK OF A WAY TO EXPLAIN HOW I GOT HERE--

ROT. I'D GIVE *ANYTHING* TO TALK TO JENNIFER! I DON'T CARE IF SHE *IS* MARRIED OR ENGAGED OR WHATEVER. SHE WAS ALWAYS A GREAT *LISTENER!*

I'M STILL TALKING TO THE CAT. ARG.

GLUG.

FROM CAT TALK TO FROG. WELL, THERE'S AN IMPROVEMENT.

MEOW?

YEAH, "*GLUG.*" THAT PRETTY WELL SUMS IT UP.

URRPP!

HEY...YOU AREN'T GOING TO *PUKE* OR ANYTHING, ARE YOU...

ROT. IF I WAS *REALLY* A SUPER-HERO I COULD FIGURE THINGS *OUT.*

SUPER-HEROES LIKE SUPERMAN AND GREEN LANTERN SEEM TO HAVE AUTOMATIC DEDUCTIVE ABILITIES RIGHT ALONG WITH THEIR POWERS.

I'VE READ ALL THE SHERLOCK HOLMES STORIES...EVERYTHING AGATHA CHRISTIE EVER WROTE ...WATCHED EVERY EPISODE OF "MURDER SHE WROTE" AND RE-RUNS OF "PERRY MASON..."

"...AND *I* STILL KEEP DEPENDING ON A GIRL I HAVEN'T *SEEN* SINCE THE JUNIOR PROM!"

THIS IS *TERRIFIC,* JEN. I ALMOST FEEL LIKE A *NORMAL* GUY!

THAT'S ALL *I* EVER WANTED, RAY...

...*NORMALCY.* IT MAY BE OLD-*FASHIONED,* BUT I WAS BROUGHT UP IN AN AWFULLY "*TRADITIONAL*" HOME...

YOU *KNOW* HOW MY MOM IS...

"HEY, *WAIT* A SECOND... '*TRADITIONAL*'... IF JENNIFER WAS *MARRIED...*

"...SHE WOULD HAVE-- '*TRADITIONALLY*' -- TAKEN HER HUSBAND'S NAME...

"BUT... WHEN I WENT TO THE BANK SHE WORKS AT, HER NAMEPLATE SAID 'JURDEN'--"

JURDEN

"AND... AND, '*TRADITIONALLY,*' SHE WOULD HAVE WORN A *WEDDING RING!* THAT'S JUST THE WAY SHE *IS!*"

THIS MEANS-- I MEAN-- IT-- IT--

--JENNIFER ISN'T MARRIED--

THIS MEANS-- JENNIFER *ISN'T* MARRIED!

RORROWL

CARL + HILDE

FFWWOOSHH

54

MUNNCHEN ABEGEBRANNT MEIN FRUHSTACHEN!

WELL, THERE BLOWS *THAT* THEORY.

I FIGURED I'D BURNED THESE FREAKY POWERS OUT.

ALL *RIGHT!* NOW BACK TO *PHILLY* AND... AND... ROT! WHICH WAY *IS* PHILADELPHIA?

I'VE NEVER BEEN MORE THAN *FIVE MILES* FROM HOME AND NOW I'VE GOT TO FIND MY WAY BACK FROM HALFWAY AROUND THE *WORLD!*

THIS IS JUST ZIPPY!

I CAN'T EVEN FOLD A *ROADMAP*...NOT THAT I EVER *NEEDED* ONE... UNTIL *NOW!*

ACTUALLY, YOU SHOULD BE AIMING FOR THE *PHILIPPINES*, WHERE YOU'RE *NEEDED.*

HUH--!?

--THE RAY!

DON'T YOU EVER READ THE *PAPERS*, SON?

I'M *NOT* YOUR SON!

THERE'S A *VOLCANO* IN THE PHILIPPINES THREATENING *THOUSANDS* ...AND *YOUR POWER* COULD SAVE THEM!

THE *REAL* MYSTERY IS HOW YOU CAN REFUSE TO USE THE GIFT OF YOUR POWERS TO HELP OTHERS.

LOOK, FIN-HEAD, THIS SUPER-HERO GIG IS *YOUR* HANG-UP! THERE'S THE *SUN* RISING IN THE EAST, SO PHILLY'S *WEST*--THIS WAY!

MY POWER IS BEING USED TO *FIND JENNIFER!*

Der Nuz DIE GEFHAR DE VULK

YEAH, RIGHT. GET REAL. NOW HOW ABOUT HELPING ME *NAVIGATE HOME*, OR IS DOING THAT A BIG MYSTERY TOO?

SEE

BUT *SHE'S* IN NO DANGER! *HOLD IT!* LISTEN TO ME--!

YOU

LATER!

MUCH

LATER,

I.

HOPE! OWCH!

KWAM!

24 HOUR TELLER

ONE WAY

Y'KNOW--I'VE REALLY *GOT* TO WORK ON MY LANDINGS --OWW--

MADE IT... BUT THOSE PANTS THE GERMAN POLICE GAVE ME *DIDN'T.* MY *BODY HEAT* MADE *ASHES* OUT OF THEM!

OW! OW! MY *NECK* HURTS AGAIN AND I'M *NAKED* IN AN ALLEY. WHAT *MORE* COULD GO WRONG?

WHY DID I ASK?

MICHAEL NESMITH'S PANTS ARE GROWING UP MY LEGS--!

KEEP OUT

I'M DOING IT! STOP COMPLAINING. YOU HAVE TO LOOK *DECENT!*

YEAH? WELL, *THESE* PANTS DON'T HELP!

HEY, KID-- WHAT'RE YOU DOIN' BACK HERE--?

WE'VE HAD SOME *TROUBLE* HERE-ABOUTS. YOU HAVE TO VACATE THIS AREA. IT'S *BANK PROPERTY!*

OH, HEY! YOU *WORK* IN THERE DON'T YOU? YOU KNOW *JENNY JURDEN?*

NO, NO. *WAIT,* OKAY? OKAY? LET ME LEAVE HER A *NOTE,* OKAY?

I JUST WANT TO JOT DOWN MY *NUMBER,* THEN I'LL GO.

I CAN'T GIVE YOU ANY *PERSONAL INFORMATION* REGARDING BANK *EMPLOYEES.* NOW *GEDDOUDAHERE.*

A...A PEN...? OH, LET ME BORROW YOUR *BALL-POINT,* OKAY?

HEY!

LOOK, GIVE THIS TO *JENNIFER JURDEN,* OKAY?

HEY, OKAY? *OKAY?*

SLAM

KEEP OUT

ROT...

RAYMOND? THE PHILIPPINES?

HEY! HE COULDN'T *SEE* YOU, COULD HE? MAYBE YOU'RE JUST SOME KIND OF *HALLUCINATION* CAUSED BY ALL MY *FLYING AROUND.*

NO, I'M VERY REAL. I HAVE TO...

I'LL TELL YOU WHAT YOU "*HAVE TO.*" YOU *HAVE TO LEAVE ME ALONE!*

57

MEANWHILE, AT RAY'S HOUSE...

HEAVENS, THIS NEIGHBORHOOD HOLDS SO MANY *MEMORIES!*

THERE'S THE *TERRILL* HOUSE... IT LOOKS *DESERTED,* BUT THEN IT ALWAYS *DID* WITH THOSE *BLACKENED* WINDOWS.

I WONDER IF RAY'S *IN* OR THAT DITZY *HANK* GUY WHO WAS THERE YESTERDAY...

THIS IS *CRAZY...* HOW COULD *RAY* HAVE ANYTHING TO DO WITH--

JENNIFER...?

YES, IT *IS* YOU. YOU'RE LITTLE *JENNY JURDEN* ALL GROWN UP, *AREN'T* YOU?

I...I REMEMBER YOU!

SISTER *ROSEMARY...* AND SISTER *MARY ROSE!*

YOU...YOU WERE RAY TERRILL'S *TEACHERS* WHEN WE WERE LITTLE!

THIS IS A REAL *COINCIDENCE!* I WAS JUST COMING TO *LOOK* FOR RAY! HE...

UM. IS...IS THAT *YOUR* VAN? IT... IT LOOKS LIKE ONE I SAW OVER AT THE *BANK.* WERE YOU *FOLLOW--?*

THE "GLUTCH" RETURNS TO JENNIFER JURDEN'S STOMACH...

...BUT ONLY FOR A MOMENT...

HUSH, DEAR. THIS IS NOT THE TIME NOR THE PLACE FOR *QUESTIONS!*

MMMMMMPH!

60

SOME MILES EAST...

CLANK

VATERCOLF PSYCHIATRIC HOSPITAL

WE'VE *ARRIVED*, MY *CHILD*.

WHERE... WHERE *ARE* WE? WHY ARE YOU *DOING* THIS?

DO NOT *FEAR*, *JENNIFER JURDEN*, YOU ARE ABOUT TO ENTER THE PRESENCE OF HIM WHO IS *ONE* WITH *THE LIGHT*...

THIS... THIS IS A *MENTAL* INSTITUTION!

OH MY... THEY'VE GONE OFF THE *DEEP END* AND THEY'RE TAKING ME *WITH* THEM!

HUH? THAT *LIGHT*...

SO... BRIGHT...

OWWW... MY *EYES*...

UHULLP! WE... WE'RE INSIDE!

WELCOME, FAVORED ONE OF *RAY TERRILL*. WELCOME TO THE HOVEL OF *CALDWELL THE CANDLE MAN!*

EXPERIENCE. NOW *FOLLOW* ME OR YOU'LL END UP LOST ON THE OTHER SIDE OF THE *WORLD* AGAIN!

HEY! *HEY!* HOW'D YOU GET *AHEAD* OF ME?

YEAH? THEN HOW ABOUT SOME *NAVIGATING* LESSONS?

LATER. WE'VE ARRIVED.

AT THE *PHILIPPINES?* BUT WE JUST LEFT *PHILLY!?*

THE SPEED OF *LIGHT* IS OURS, RAY. GET USED TO IT AND LEARN TO MINIMIZE YOUR VELOCITY.

≳KKAPH≴ ROT, THE AIR'S FULL OF *HOT ASH!* I... UNNN... HEY, I FEEL KIND OF WOOZY...

THERE IT IS. THE REPORTS SAID IT'S GOING TO BLOW AT ANY SECOND.

RAY! *RAY!*

THE ASH IS BLOCKING THE *SUN!*

YOU'RE *EXHAUSTING* YOUR POWER!

T-TELL ME SOMETHING I DON'T KNOOOOWW!

WHOAAAA!

THE *LAVA!* PULL ENERGY FROM THE *LAVA!* YOU CAN USE *ANY* NATURAL LIGHT SOURCE TO RECHARGE!

UNNN-- AHHH!

WOW!

POOM

IT *WORKED!*

WHAT A *RUSH!*

64

KWAMM

OOPS!

"OOPS," INDEED! ALL YOU DID WAS *FEED THE FIRE!* AS I *SAID,* WE HAVE TO *PLAN* OUR MOVES!

LOOK DOWN THERE! THE U.S. *MILITARY BASE* HAS BEEN *EVACUATED...*

WE HAVE TO STOP THIS THING FOR *THEM!* YOUR *RECKLESSNESS* IS THREATENING THEIR *LIVES.*

YEAH, OKAY, SORRY... KEEPING YOUR *HOME.* I CAN SEE HOW THAT CAN BE A REAL PRIORITY.

UH-OH...

PRETTY *NEAT,* HUH?

66

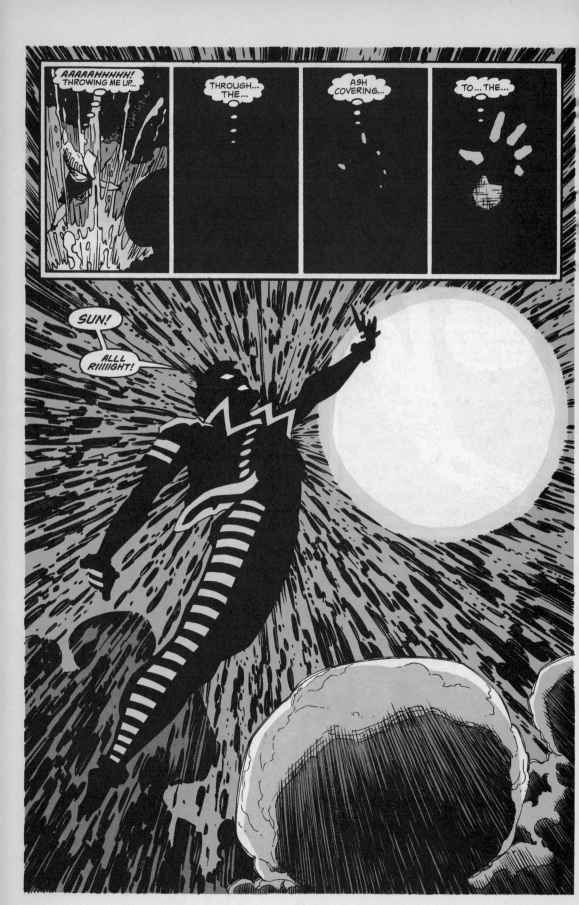

SEE, JENNIFER JURDEN? DO YOU SEE THE POWER YOUR FRIEND NOW WIELDS? AND WITH SUCH POWER COMES GREAT OBLIGATION.

IT'S UNBELIEVABLE...

EXCELLENT, RAYMOND. EXCELLENT!

THE ERUPTION AT SEA WILL CAUSE GREAT WAVES, BUT THE MOUNTAIN WILL SHIELD THE LAND. YOU DID--

STUFF IT!

POW!

UNNGH!

WHAT-- THE DEVIL--

YOU'RE A LIAR! IF YOU WERE... WERE "IMMATERIAL," LIKE YOU SAID, HOW COULD A CHUNK OF LAVA KNOCK YOU SILLY?

I WASN'T NEEDED HERE! YOU COULD HAVE HANDLED IT ALL! YOU HAVE THE POWER AND THE EXPERIENCE.

WHAT'S YOUR REAL REASON BEHIND TRYING TO FORCE ME INTO BEING A SUPER-HERO? WHO ARE YOU REALLY!

69

KRAAKK-

VATER **PSYCH** **HOSE**

BOOOM!

FOUND MY WAY EASY ENOUGH...

HUH? IT'S A *NUT* HOUSE! WHY WOULD JEN BE...

RAY?

JEN! YES! IT...IT'S *ME!* DON'T BE *AFRAID,* OKAY? IT'S JUST *ME.*

I... I KNOW, RAY...

HEY! I WON'T *HURT* YOU, JEN. I KNOW THIS IS ALL *CRAZY,* BUT I'M STILL *ME...*

NO... NO YOU'RE NOT! I'VE LEARNED SO *MUCH,* RAY...

I'VE LEARNED ALL *ABOUT* YOU... MORE THAN EVEN *YOU* KNOW AS YET!

AND I KNOW WHAT YOU HAVE TO *DO!* AND I CAN'T... *NO ONE* CAN BE ANY PART OF IT!

YOU... YOU HAVE TO DO IT *ALONE!*

ALONE? DO *WHAT* ALONE? JENNY, *DON'T GO!*

--DON'T--

71

HE IS FREE.

SUSPENDED ABOVE THE TURBULENT OCEAN, HE *UNLEASHES* HIS POWER.

HE FEELS THE VERY FORCES OF NATURE *OOZE* THROUGH HIS FINGERS.

HE FEELS THEM *DISCHARGE* IN THE AIR AROUND HIM AT HIS COMMAND.

HE *REJOICES* AS WIND AND WAVES WHIP IN FURY AROUND HIM.

HE IS FREE.

GOD HELP US ALL.

LIES.

THEY THOUGHT THEY COULD HOLD ME...LOCK ME *AWAY*...

WELL, THEY WERE WRONG!!!

NOTHING CAN --ARRRAAGH!

KX-RAKK

TIME PASSES...

UHH...?

WHAT...? OH *NO*, LOOK WHAT HE'S DONE *NOW*--A TORNADO!

NO...NO... HOW LONG WAS I *OUT*? I *CAN'T* HAVE MISSED MY BUS!

BUS STOP

GOOD... GOOD. MY GEAR'S STILL THERE!

I'VE *GOT* TO REACH *PHILLY* SOON AND FIND OUT WHO WAS RESPONSIBLE FOR THIS!

FREAK MELTS VAN!

PHOTO BY LOU FINE

MELTED THE VAN...

...GREAT HEAT...

...HE GENERATED HEAT...

...AND SUCH HEAT COULD DESTROY HIM...

...AND *SAVE* EVERYONE ELSE!

SOMEWHERE BETWEEN WILMINGTON, DELAWARE AND PHILADELPHIA, PENNSYLVANIA...

IT'S NOT FAIR! IT'S *NOT*!!

I'VE LOVED JENNIFER... WANTED HER FOR SO MANY YEARS! AND, WHEN I'M FINALLY ABLE TO *DO* SOMETHING ABOUT IT...

...SHE SLAMS THE DOOR ON ME!

--AND INSTANTLY DEVELOP THE LIGHT-BASED *SUPER-POWERS* DAD WAS SO AFRAID OF!

POWERS THAT HAVE *DERAILED* MY ENTIRE LIFE!

ALL THOSE YEARS MY DAD LIED TO ME-- TOLD ME I WAS ALLERGIC TO SUNLIGHT--KEPT ME ISOLATED INDOORS--

--JENNIFER JURDEN WAS MY ONLY FRIEND!

ONCE MY DAD...DIED... CONFESSING HIS LIE TO ME JUST BEFORE... I WAS FREE TO GO OUT IN THE LIGHT--

NOW SOME NUTCASE CLAIMING TO BE MY *REAL* FATHER HAUNTS ME DAY AND NIGHT-- CLAIMS HE AND I ARE BOTH... ALIENS...

...SURE WOULD EXPLAIN A LOT... I'VE ALWAYS FELT LIKE A STRANGER IN A STRANGE LAND...

NOW JEN KNOWS SOMETHING THAT'S CONVINCED HER WE CAN NEVER SEE EACH OTHER!

SOMETHING ALONG THE LINES OF "NEVER WITH MARTIANS," I'LL BET--

RAYMOND--

77

79

I'VE *ACED* THIS FLYING ROUTINE! I'M MOVING SO FAST NO ONE CAN EVEN *SEE* ME COME HOME! I...

FOR SALE
SUN REALTY
215·555

RING! RING! RING!

EH!?

HELLO? HELLO?

REAL *SPEEDY*, TERRILL. YOU CAN MOVE AS FAST AS *LIGHT* AND YOU *STILL* MISS PHONE CALLS.

SLAM

TIME TO GIVE THE RAY'S LIGHT CONFIGURATION TRICK THE ACID TEST...

...*FINALLY*, SOME *REAL* CLOTHES. WHAT DO YOU KNOW... OL' FINHEAD'S GOOD FOR SOMETHING AFTER ALL.

THIS SI
UP

HEY! WHAT THE *DEUCE*? ALL MY STUFF'S BEEN *PACKED AWAY!* WHAT THE DING DONG'S COMING *DOWN?*

O.P.P.
TERRILL
12
FRAGILE
FRAGILE
THIS SIDE UP
GLASSWARE
THIS SIDE UP
GLASSWA

KRIPES! THE WHOLE *HOUSE* IS IN BOXES... AND... *ROT!* A *"FOR SALE"* SIGN! AND, GREAT, HERE'S THAT *BRETT* GUY...

AH, *RAYMOND!* WAS THAT SOME KIND OF *GAG* YOU PULLED EARLIER? CALLING ME AND SAYING YOU WERE ON THE OTHER SIDE OF THE *WORLD?*

FOR SALE
SUN REALTY
215-555-5478

ARRROOOOO
...OOOO·

EMERSON WAS *RIGHT!*
THE BEING WHO GENERATES
SUCH HEAT IS A
POTENTIAL *DANGER*... HE MIGHT
INDEED HAVE BEEN ABLE TO
HELP EMERSON BE RID OF
ME...

BUT
IT'S *TOO LATE*
NOW... I'LL SEE
WHOEVER DID *THIS*
DESTROYED *FIRST!*

LOOK AT ALL THIS
STUFF... WHO'D BELIEVE
IT BELONGS TO
SUPER-POWERED BEINGS
FROM SOME OTHER
PLANET...

FOR SALE
SUN REALTY
15·555·5478

83

YOU KNOW, IT'S ALL JUST *COME* TO ME. YOU *KNOW* TOO MUCH!

YOU KNEW ABOUT MY *POWERS*... YOU KNEW ABOUT THE *OLD RAY*...

YOU'VE BEEN PRESSING ME TO MAKE SOME KIND OF *SUPER-HERO* OUT OF MYSELF JUST LIKE HIM!

AND THE BIG YELLOW GOOF *SAID* HIS POWERS *RETARD* THE AGING PROCESS...

IT ALL *FITS*, "HANK," IT ALL *FITS*!

ADMIT IT! YOU'RE *HIM*! *YOU'RE* THE RAY!

THE ONLY THING THAT FITS, G, IS...

POW!

THIS! RIGHT IN YOUR GAUDY GREEN EYE!

FRAGILE

THIS SIDE UP

PLATES

HANDLE WITH CARE

HANDLE WITH CARE

THIS SIDE UP

PERSONAL ITEMS

PER ITE

OWW!

...THEN AGAIN, I COULD BE MISTAKEN...

...NOT ANOTHER BLACK EYE...

THIS SIDE

THE SIDE UP

DUDE BE *TRIPPIN'!*

RAY? I HOPE YOU DON'T MIND MY USING OUR OLD "PRIVATE ENTRANCE." I HAD TO--OH! WHAT... WHAT'S HAPPENED?

FRAGILE

THIS SIDE UP

"WHAT'S HAPPENED?" NOW, THERE'S A LOADED QUESTION!

DO YOU WANT ME TO BEGIN WITH THE OTHER DAY, WHEN I WAS BORN OR WHEN I LANDED?

RAY, RAY... EVEN IN YOUR DARKEST DAYS AS A KID YOU NEVER SOUNDED SO BITTER...

I...I'VE COME TO HELP YOU. I DON'T CARE WHAT EVERYONE'S TOLD ME. I THINK YOU NEED SOMEONE AT YOUR SIDE.

OUTER SPACE? WHAT ARE YOU TALKING ABOUT?

ISN'T THAT WHAT YOU LEARNED ABOUT ME... THAT I'M FROM ANOTHER PLANET? THAT I'M AN ALIEN?

AT MY SIDE? AREN'T YOU AFRAID OF MY... MY POWERS? AREN'T YOU AFRAID OF BEING THE FRIEND OF AN ALIEN FROM OUTER SPACE?

AN ALIEN? HA HA HA HA HA HA!

OH, RAY, THEY JUST TOLD YOU THAT SO YOU'D STAY AWAY FROM ME!

THEY DIDN'T WANT YOU DISTRACTED FROM YOUR MISSION! YOU'RE AS HUMAN AS I AM.

LET ME PROVE IT!

MMMMMM ...??

"NOW THE *TRUTH,* SON: IT BEGAN IN 1939 WHEN A *DR. DAYZL* ORGANIZED A GROUP OF FELLOW SCIENTISTS TO STUDY...*LIGHT...*

"BACKED BY A DEFENSE-ANXIOUS U.S. GOVERNMENT, THEY FORMED A PROJECT--*RESEARCH ON THE PROPERTIES OF LIGHT,* CODE-NAMED *RONOL...*"

THEY ACHIEVED *REMARKABLE* PROGRESS, DISCOVERING, FOR EXAMPLE, VERSIONS OF THE LASER *DECADES* BEFORE ITS OFFICIALLY RECOGNIZED DEVELOPMENT...

BUT ULTIMATELY, THE GOVERNMENT PUT ITS FAITH IN *ATOMIC* RESEARCH.

"THEY *DISBANDED* THE GROUP AND MANY MEMBERS JOINED THE *MANHATTAN PROJECT,* WHICH DEVELOPED THE FIRST ATOMIC BOMB...

RONOL LAB

"THEY SAID THAT ACTION *BROKE* DAYZL.

"HE BEGAN TO BELIEVE THAT *LIGHT*...THE *SUBJECT* OF HIS LIFE'S WORK... WAS NOT JUST RADIANT *ENERGY,* BUT AN *INTELLIGENCE* DANGEROUS TO ALL MANKIND..."

MY FATHER'S SCRAPBOOK... THERE'S A *"RONOL"* STAMP ON IT...

EXACTLY! NOW, WE MUST ACCELERATE...

WHAT'S IT ALL HAVE TO DO WITH US...WITH ME...? I--*WHOOOOP!*

WHAT WAS *THAT?* HEY! HEY! HEY! I'M OUT OF *POWWWWWWWWEEEERRRRRRRRRRRRRRRRR!!*

UMMPH! MAN, BILLY PENN, I AM *SO GLAD* THE CITY FATHERS PUT YOU HERE!

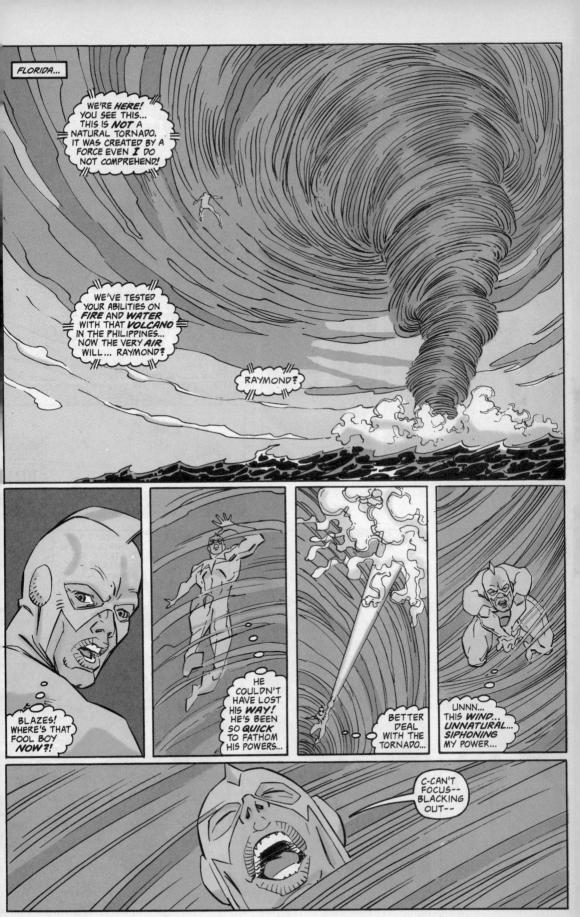

POLARIS... POLARIS...

HEY, HEY, HOLD THE PHONE! YOU'RE THAT *MAGNET* GUY WHO'S GOT IT IN FOR *GREEN LANTERN!*

WHY THE HECK ARE YOU LAYING FOR *ME?!* I DON'T EVEN *KNOW* THE GUY...

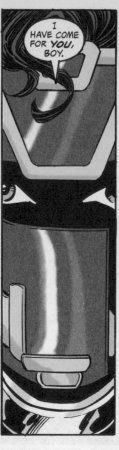

I HAVE COME FOR *YOU,* BOY.

RUN. FIGHT. RUN. KICK BUTT. RUN. DECLARE WAR. WET YOURSELF.

GOTTA WORK ON MY WAR CRIES...

NOT A *MISTER,* CHANCE!!

I MUST USE MY *MAGNETIC BLACK HOLE FORCE BEAM* TO *DRAW OUT* YOUR POWER, BOY. YOU POSE A POTENTIAL *THREAT...*

OWCH!

WE MUST ENDEAVOR TO END THIS *QUICKLY!*

HE... HE... WITH JUST A WAVE OF HIS HAND...

...THAT'S... SO COOL...

...EXCEPT THAT THIS LUNATIC'S TRYIN' TO *WASTE* ME!!!

WHERE'S THAT *RAY* GEEK WHEN YOU *NEED* HIM?!

GOTTA... GOTTA CALL THE *COPS...* THE *ARMY!!*

AAARRHHH!

EMERSON WAS *RIGHT* ABOUT YOUR POWER-- YOU'RE *TOO* DANGEROUS TO LIVE!

GOTTA GET TO A LOWER LEDGE BEFORE HE RECOVERS...

AND WHO THE *HECK* IS EMERSON?

PREPARE TO *DIE*, STRIPLING-- THAT *POLARIS* MIGHT *LIVE!!*

NO DOUBT IN *MY* MIND...

...*THIS* IS A JOB FOR *SUPERMAN!*

94

95

THE RAY

EMERSON MUST DIE

EMERSON WANTS TO SAVE THE WORLD.

HE WANTS TO PROTECT US ALL FROM HIS DEADLY ALTER EGO, DR. POLARIS.

SO, EMERSON BROUGHT POLARIS TO FLORIDA, AND SOUGHT TO USE THE SERENE ENVIRONS TO IMPRISON POLARIS WITHIN EMERSON'S MIND.

BUT POLARIS ESCAPED.

THE RAY FOUGHT A LOSING BATTLE WITH A VIOLENT TORNADO WHICH WAS BORN OF DR. POLARIS' MANIPULATION OF THE EARTH'S MAGNETIC FIELD.

NOW THE RAY IS HELPLESS TO PREVENT POLARIS FROM DESTROYING THE ONE BEING WHO STANDS BETWEEN POLARIS AND EMERSON--

WAIT A FREAKIN' *MINUTE.* I CONNECTED BEFORE WHEN HE WAS NORMAL-SIZED! WHY'S HE PLAYING LIKE A *PHANTOM ECONOMY* SIZED? SOMETHING NOT QUITE RIGHT HERE...

YEAH! YEAH! I *THOUGHT* SO! THE CREEP'S PROJECTING AN *ILLUSION!*

IF I *SQUINT,* I CAN SEE THE *REAL* DR. POLARIS RIGHT ABOUT...

...*THERE!*

ZAPPED HIM! FINE. I GET AN EXTRA *LIFE* AND MOVE *UP* A LEVEL. *NOW* WHAT?

ARRRAGH!

OKAY, OKAY. HE...HE'S OUT *COLD* --FOR A MOMENT... GIVES ME A CHANCE TO THINK. LET'S SEE, WHAT HAVE I *READ* ABOUT DR. POLARIS...

DR. POLARIS: MASTER OF MAGNETISM

Photo by Lou Fine

EN LANTERN

YEAH, YEAH, I REMEMBER. HE'S A MAJOR SUPER-BADDIE. AND HE'S AFRAID OF *MY* POWER?!

WHOA! HE'S--

YOU'RE *RESOURCEFUL* FOR ONE SO YOUNG. YOU SHOULD NOT BE PERMITTED TO GET ANY *OLDER!*

OWWWW! OW! STOP IT!

99

LOOK-- YOU WIN, OKAY? FINE. I WON'T TRY TO STOP YOU FROM X-ING THIS "EMERSON" GUY--

--NOW, GO BOTHER SOMEBODY ELSE, OKAY --?

MEDDLESOME FOOL! EMERSON SOUGHT YOU OUT THAT YOU MIGHT USE YOUR LIGHT TO DESTROY ME! EMERSON HAS EXPOSED YOU AS THE THREAT YOU TRULY ARE!

I SHALL NOT REST UNTIL I HAVE SQUEEZED THE LIFE FROM YOU!!

NOOO!!!

ZZZAAAPP!!

THAT'S TWICE I'VE BLOWN IT WITH THIS GUY!

WAIT! I GOT IT! THIS IS OBVIOUSLY ANOTHER ONE OF RAY'S STUPID TESTS!

LOOK, I DON'T WANT TO HURT YOU, BUT I'M GETTING A LITTLE TIRED OF HAVING THE POWER SUCKED OUT OF ME!

SO, JUST DIME UP OL' FINHEAD AND LET'S CALL IT A NIGHT!

TEST?

TESTING YOU IS NOT MY AIM, STRIPLING--

--DESTROYING YOU IS!!

OW.

OW.

OW.

OW.

OW.

ROT! IS THAT WHAT I THINK IT IS--?

AH! I SEE WHAT THE BOY FEARS! THE *SUNSET!*

EACH TIME THE POWER IS DRAWN FROM HIM HE CAN RENEW-- AS LONG AS HE CAN REACH THE SUNLIGHT.

BUT IF HE CANNOT...

C'MON... C'MON... *BUILD!!* ONE BURST OF LIGHT SPEED AND I CAN LOSE THIS BOZO!

OWCH! NOW HE'S THROWING *ROCKS?* NO. NO. THEY'RE *MAGNETIZED.* MUST HAVE *IRON* IN 'EM AND HE'S TOSSING THEM WITH HIS *POWER!*

GOT TO GET OUT OF THESE *SHADOWS* AND...

RE...

...CHARGE!

ARRRAAGH!

THE BOY IS RESOURCEFUL. HE WILL BE ABLE TO FACE THE COMING DISAS--

WHAT THE DING DONG IS GOING ON IN HERE!?

OH. YES. WELL, THIS IS CALDWELL. HE CALLS HIMSELF CALDWELL THE CANDLEMAN.

REALLY? WELL, IF THE STATE IS GOING TO CONTINUE TO CALL ME FRED THE FIRE INSPECTOR, SOMETHING'S GOT TO CHANGE IN HERE!

THE CANDLES ARE PART OF HIS THERAPY.

NO...

SORRY, DOC. AGAINST THE CODE.

YOU CANNOT! THIS MUST NOT BE! I MUST MONITOR THE BOY'S PROGRESS!

MONITORING BOYS IS AGAINST THE CODE.

GIVE ME A HAND HERE, WILL YA, DOC? I PROMISE YOU CAN MAKE A FEW BIRTHDAY WISHES IF YA WANT, PHFFFFF!

NO! NO! MY LIGHTS! MY LIGHTS!

THE TERRILL HOUSE...

I GUESS BEING INVOLVED WITH A *SUPER-HERO* IS LIKE DATING A *DOCTOR*...

...YOU SPEND A LOT OF TIME SITTING AROUND *WAITING*.

WELL, I CAN'T *DO* THAT. I HAVE *STUDYING* TO DO AND *WORK* TO GET READY FOR. I GUESS I CAN...

OH, UM, HI! IF YOU'RE LOOKING FOR *RAY TERRILL*, HE ISN'T HOME.

I'M *NATHANIEL BRETT*, MR. TERRILL'S *ATTORNEY*. WHO ARE YOU?

OH, I'M *JENNIFER JURDEN* ...A FRIEND.

REALLY? WELL IF *YOU* CAN EVER REACH THE BOY, GIVE HIM *THIS*! IT'S THE *LEASE* TO HIS NEW *APARTMENT*.

LEASE?

YES. HE'S *MOVING OUT* OF HERE TODAY. COME ON, BOYS.

BLAKE'S
MOVING AND STORAGE

MEOW.

HOW AM I GOING TO FIND *RAY* NOW AND *TELL* HIM...

SISTER **ROSEMARY!**

OH, JENNIFER, WE NEED YOUR **HELP!** RAYMOND NEEDS YOUR HELP!

WE HAVE **LOST CONTACT** WITH **CALDWELL** AND **HE** HAS LOST CONTACT WITH RAYMOND! AND THE DANGER... OH, THE DANGER IS SO VERY **CLOSE!**

WILL YOU COME?

UM... OKAY. OKAY. BUT I DON'T SEE HOW **I** CAN HELP--

THAT GIRL! THAT **GIRL!** SHE WAS THE ONE INVOLVED IN THAT WEIRD **ROBBERY** THE OTHER DAY AT FIRST FEDERAL...

WHAT IS SHE HANGING AROUND THE **TERRILL** HOUSE FOR?

MAN, BILLINGS. IF THIS ISN'T THE BEGINNING OF A **GREAT NEWS STORY** THEN **NOTHING** IS! I'M **TAILING** HER!

THE NUNS TAKE JENNIFER AND THAT REPORTER TAKES OFF AFTER THE NUNS?

LOOKS LIKE I WOKE UP JUST IN TIME...

LEAVE ME ALONE, YOU JERK!! I'VE DONE NOTHING TO YOU!!

MAYBE HE'LL TAKE A HINT--

--O FOR 4, TERRILL...

THIS HAS GONE FAR ENOUGH, WHELP!

AS THE SUN IS OBVIOUSLY YOUR POWER SOURCE, I SHALL DEPRIVE YOU OF ITS RAYS--

--AND CRUSH YOU WITHIN THE EARTH'S WOMB!

I'LL SAY THIS FOR HIM, HE'S GOT THE RAP DOWN COLD!

MY DINKY FORCE FIELD WON'T HOLD OUT FOREVER...WITHOUT THE SUN TO CHARGE UP ON, MY ENERGY DRAINS OUT LIKE A YEAR-OLD ENERGIZER!

MAN... THIS... HURTS...

GETTING... HARD TO BREATHE...

ROT... LOSING THE HELMET... IT'S ONLY A LIGHT CONSTRUCT... FORCE FIELD COLLAPSING ON IT--

--J--JENNIFER--!

THE VATERCOLF PSYCHIATRIC HOSPITAL...

YOU *LEARNED*, JENNIFER...

YOU WERE SHOWN HOW CALDWELL WAS *ONE* WITH THE LIGHT...

...HOW HE COULD *COMMUNICATE* THROUGH THE CANDLE FLAMES.

...HOW HE *WATCHES OVER* RAY TERRILL AND *GUIDES* HIM TOWARDS HIS DESTINY.

BUT NOW YOU SEE, JENNIFER? THERE IS *NO LIGHT* FROM CALDWELL'S ROOM...

THEY HAVE *EXTINGUISHED* HIS CANDLES... *SNUFFED* OUT THE LIGHT.

MOVED HIM TO WE KNOW NOT WHERE... AND THE DANGER RAYMOND FACES GROWS SO MUCH CLOSER. *HELP* HIM, JENNIFER...

"*YOU* CAN FIND CALDWELL..."

RECEPTION

GOOD EVENING. MAY I HELP YOU?

UM...YES. MY NAME IS, UM... JENNIFER *CALDWELL*. I'M LOOKING FOR MY, UM... *UNCLE*...

MEANWHILE...

OKAY, I GIVE. I BLEW IT.

I'M NO SUPER-HERO. UNNN... TRAINING'S OVER...

COME ON, LET ME GO. I FAILED THE TEST. GIVE ME AN 'F'...

OKAY, RAY, YOU CAN CALL OFF YOUR BOY!

RAY?

C'MON, FINHEAD, CHILL OUT-- I CAN'T...KEEP THIS FIELD UP... MUCH LONGER...

IT'S AS THOUGH...AS IF... HE'S REALLY... HE'S...

...OH, DIP...

...HE'S *REALLY* TRYING TO KILL ME!

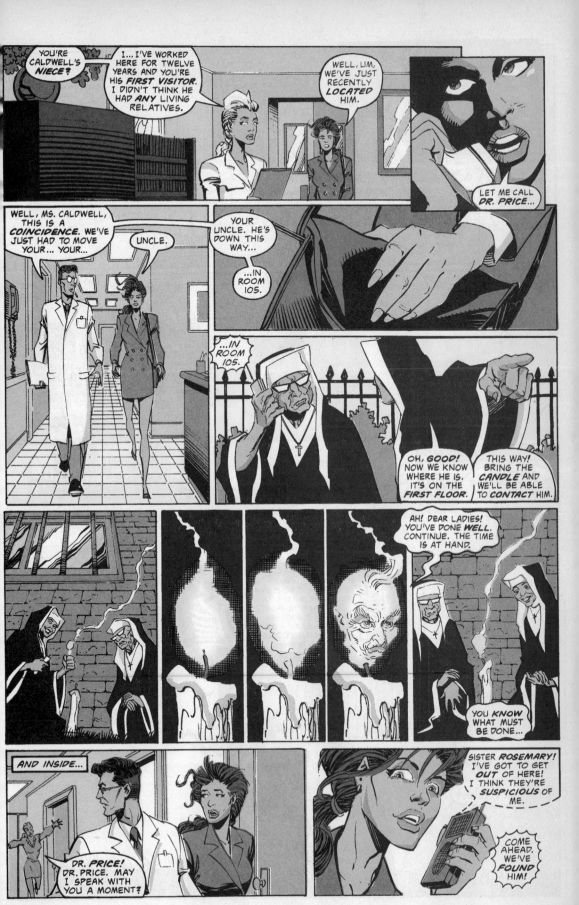

109

SAVE IT, BIG BIRD. I'M NOT BUYING.

--PURE, DUMB LUCK. PERIOD. IT'S A MIRACLE I'M STILL BREATHING.

THIS CREEP'S GOT THE ABILITY TO CONTROL THE MAGNETIC FORCE OF THE EARTH! HE CAN EVEN OPEN UP BLACK HOLES--

YOU MEAN, THIS MAN ATTACKED YOU-- WAS ABLE TO PICK YOU OUT OF THE SKY WHILE YOU WERE FLYING AT NEAR LIGHT SPEED--

--AND YOU BEAT HIM HANDS DOWN? WHY, THAT'S--

MAGNETIC? BLACK HOLES! WAIT A MINUTE! WAIT A MINUTE!

YOU'RE RIGHT. EVEN WHILE HE'S OUT COLD, HE'S STILL GENERATING WAVES AND WAVES OF MAGNETIC FORCE...

LOOK AT HIM! FOCUS AND YOU CAN SEE THEM.

DO YOU REALIZE WHAT THIS MEANS? IF WE COULD CHANNEL HIS POWER, HE COULD OPEN A GATEWAY TO THE LIGHT ENTITY AS EASILY AS CALDWELL!

THE WHAT? WHAT GATEWAY? AND WHAT'S A 'LIGHT ENTITY'? AND WHO'S 'CALDWELL'?

IT'S...IT'S YOUR MISSION, RAY. IT'S THE REASON I BECAME THE RAY AND THE REASON YOU WERE BORN!

ONLY ONE WHO WAS BORN WITH THE LIGHT, AS YOU WERE, CAN COMMUNICATE WITH THE LIGHT ENTITY AND WAYLAY ITS COLLISION COURSE WITH EARTH. IT'S THE REASON BEHIND EVERYTHING!

Y'KNOW, I'VE ABOUT HAD IT WITH THIS LOONEY TRIP, BANANA BOY--

111

YOU LISTEN TO *ME*, BOY. THE FATE OF THIS *PLANET* RESTS ON YOUR NARROW SHOULDERS.

IT'S TIME TO GROW UP.

THE LIGHT ENTITY IS *RETURNING* TO EARTH. THIS *CANNOT BE ALLOWED* TO HAPPEN. ONLY YOU CAN...

BOY! YOU IN THE BLACK JACKET! CAN YOU *SEE* ME? CAN YOU *HEAR* ME?!

FORT BLISS

MY NAME IS *EMERSON*... I'M THE *TRUE PERSONA* OF DR. POLARIS...

I'VE BEEN *WATCHING*...BEEN *AWARE* OF WHAT POLARIS TRIED TO *DO* TO YOU...

FORT BLISS

HE HAS GOOD REASON TO *FEAR* YOU. I *KNEW* YOU HAD THE POWER TO *EXPUNGE* HIM FROM ME. THAT'S WHY I *SOUGHT* YOU OUT...

GEE, THANKS.

BUT DR. POLARIS IS TOO *POWERFUL*. HE *SUBDUED* ME, TOOK OVER. I CAME FOR YOUR *HELP*, BUT HE CAME TO *KILL* YOU... TO PREVENT YOU FROM SAVING *ME*!

"EMERSON MUST DIE," HUH?

RAYMOND?

HE'LL COME *BACK* IF YOU DON'T ACT *NOW!* FOCUS ON THE *MAGNETIC WAVE PATTERNS* EMANATING FROM HIS BRAIN, WHICH MAKE UP HIS *PERSONALITY*. YOU CAN *SEE* THEM! BURN THEM *OUT!* HURRY!

RAYMOND! ARE YOU *LISTENING* TO ME?

"HE BELIEVED THAT COUNTLESS EONS AGO, A *BEING OF LIGHT* WAS FORMED AT THE SAME TIME *EARTH ITSELF* WAS CREATED."

REMEMBER, RAY, HOW I TOLD YOU ABOUT THE *BRILLIANT DR. DAYZL* AND HIS THEORY REGARDING LIGHT?

"IT WAS THE *40'S* AND I WAS AS YOUNG AND AS BRASH AS YOU ARE NOW."

"WHEN *'DISASTER'* BEFELL THE BALLOON, I VOLUNTEERED TO GO OUT AND SEE WHAT COULD BE DONE."

"IT WAS *WARTIME*, AND I USED THOSE POWERS TO HELP THE WAR EFFORT AND LATER TO BATTLE THE CRIMINAL ELEMENT AT HOME."

"*UNKNOWN* TO ME, I WAS *CONSTANTLY MONITORED* BY *DAYZL*."

RAY

RAY

RAY

"IN 1950, DAYZL DROPPED FROM SIGHT AND WAS PRESUMED DEAD. WHEN HIS FILES WERE *UNSEALED*, I LEARNED HOW THAT 'COSMIC STORM' WAS REALLY A *RADIANT FLARE*..."

DE-CLASSIFIED

"...SPECIFICALLY CREATED BY *DAYZL* TO *ALTER MY GENETIC MAKE-UP*."

"SO THEORIZED THAT, 'LIGHT ENTITY' NAVIGATED THE ...SE, IT BECAME A ...ENT BEING, BENT ...TURNING TO ITS ...E;' THE EARTH.

"THE ONLY WAY TO STOP THIS BEING FROM ATTEMPTING TO OCCUPY THE SPACE THAT EARTH NOW HOLDS, DAZYL BELIEVED, WAS TO COMMUNICATE WITH IT.

"AND THE ONLY KIND OF BEING CAPABLE OF THAT WAS ONE 'BORN ONE WITH THE LIGHT.'

"ON THE PRETENSE OF 'STUDYING THE UPPER ATMOSPHERE,' DR. DAYZL'S FOLLOWERS INVITED A REPORTER ALONG TO WITNESS THEIR DISCOVERIES.

"I WAS THAT REPORTER.

"IT WAS THEN THAT I WAS EXPOSED TO A 'COSMIC STORM' WHICH ENDOWED ME WITH THE POWERS OF...THE RAY.

"I VOWED TO QUIT THEN, WHEN I REALIZED I HAD BEEN A PAWN OF A MAN I'D ONCE CONSIDERED CRAZY.

"BUT UNCLE SAM CONVINCED ME TO JOIN HIM AND THE OTHERS... HUMAN BOMB, PHANTOM LADY, DOLL MAN AND THE BLACK CONDOR AS... THE FREEDOM FIGHTERS, AT LEAST FOR A WHILE."

BUT WHEN YOU WERE BORN, RAY, I REALIZED DAYZL'S GENETIC THEORIES WERE CORRECT...

...AND I REALIZED HE WAS PROBABLY RIGHT ABOUT EVERYTHING ELSE TOO.

I CAN'T CONTROL THEM!

BWAAAMM!

A WOODED AREA NEAR THE VATERCOLF HOSPITAL...

YOU HAVE DONE *WELL*, DEAR LADIES. I HAVE SAFELY *TRANSPORTED* THROUGH THE WALLS OF MY CONFINEMENT TO THIS *RING OF LIGHT* YOU'VE MADE...

NOW CONCENTRATE... AND WE SHALL WITNESS AN OPENING... TO A REALM CLOSED TO OUR EYES SINCE THE DAWN OF TIME...

IT'S BEAUTIFUL...

ALL RIGHT, YOU PYROMANIACS! HANDS UP WHERE WE CAN SEE 'EM!

SECONDS AGO... OR MAYBE EONS
...RAY TERRILL WAS ON HIS WAY
TO SAVE THE WORLD.

BUT HE WAS *INTERRUPTED* WHEN
A TORMENTED MAN WITH DUAL
PERSONALITIES LOST CONTROL
OF HIS POWERS AND HURLED RAY
INTO THE INFINITE!

BUT THE FATE OF THE WORLD
STILL RESTS IN HIS HANDS.
IT IS UP TO HIM TO BRING
ABOUT EVERLASTING
DARKNESS OR THE...

124

127

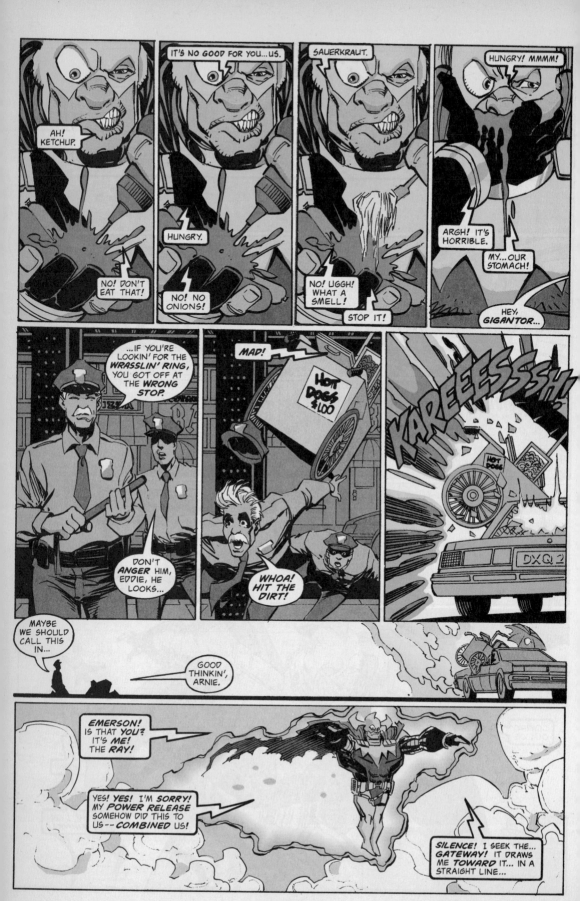

ELSEWHERE AND WHEN...

YEAH, YEAH. THIS IS JUST A DREAM, I KNOW! I'M FLYING WITHOUT USING ANY ENERGY AND MY HOUSE KEEPS GETTING FARTHER AND FARTHER AWAY!

NOW I KNOW HOW JIMMY STEWART FELT IN "VERTIGO"!

BUT WHO CARES? I'LL WAKE UP OR REALIZE I'M DEAD AND THIS WILL ALL BE...

...OVER! ULP!

JENNY! I'VE FOUND YOU!

WELCOME HOME, RAY!

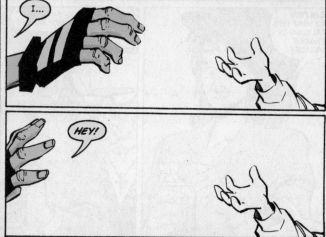

I...

HEY!

YOU AIN'T GOIN' HOME, G!

HANK --!?

MOVE OUT OF THE WAY, HANK. YOU'RE NOT MESSING UP MY DREAM LIKE YOU DID MY LIFE!

RA-AY! COME O-ON! YOU'RE GONNA BE LATE!

BEAT IT, KID!

THIS AIN'T COMPLETELY A DREAM, G! IT'S YOUR HEAD!

HEY!

BOP!

YOU'RE **BENT!** YOU'VE **ALWAYS** BEEN CRAZY! WHY DO I KEEP **LISTENING** TO YOU?

'CAUSE YOU KNOW I'M **RIGHT!** THIS LIGHT ENTITY --IT'S USING YOUR **MIND** AS A **TRANSLATOR!** IT SEES **HOME** AS **EARTH!** YOU LEAD IT **IN** THERE AND WE **ALL** GET GAFFLED!

COME ON, RAY! MR. BO-BO THE CLOWN'S WAITING AND THERE'S CAKE AND ICE CREAM AND GAMES N' STUFF!

KLAK KLAK

OH, I GET IT... YOU'RE PART OF THIS STUPID HALLUCINATION!

CLOCK IT, G! YOU'RE COMIN' BACK WITH ME!

I CAN'T LET YOU GO...

...HOME?

OUT OF MY WAY, BUTT HEAD!

HONK HONK

GREAT. NOW THIS LIGHT ENTITY'S SCRAMBLING **MY** BRAIN.

GOT TO STOP HIM...

GANGWAY! COMIN' THROUGH!

YAY RAY!

IT DOES NOT GO WELL...

RAYMOND IS *TOO FAR* INTO THE LIGHT REALM. HENRY CANNOT REACH HIS REASON!

WHAT DO YOU *MEAN?* HOW CAN YOU *TELL?*

THE ENTITY IS *SEDUCING* HIM, COMPELLING HIM TO LEAD IT *HERE!*

CALDWELL! WE'RE HAVING DIFFICULTY HOLDING BACK *POLARIS!* *FINISH* THIS! *HURRY!*

I AM *POWERLESS!* ALL HOPE LIES WITH *RAYMOND* NOW... IF ONLY HE CAN *DETER* THE ENTITY FROM *DESTROYING US ALL!*

DESTROY? DESTROY? *YES!* YESYESYESYESYESYES!

DESTROY YOU ALL!

FWAMM

DEATH TO THE FOES OF THE GREAT GOD OF LIGHT--!!

⸘KOFF KOFF⸘ ALL IS LOST! ALL IS--!

136

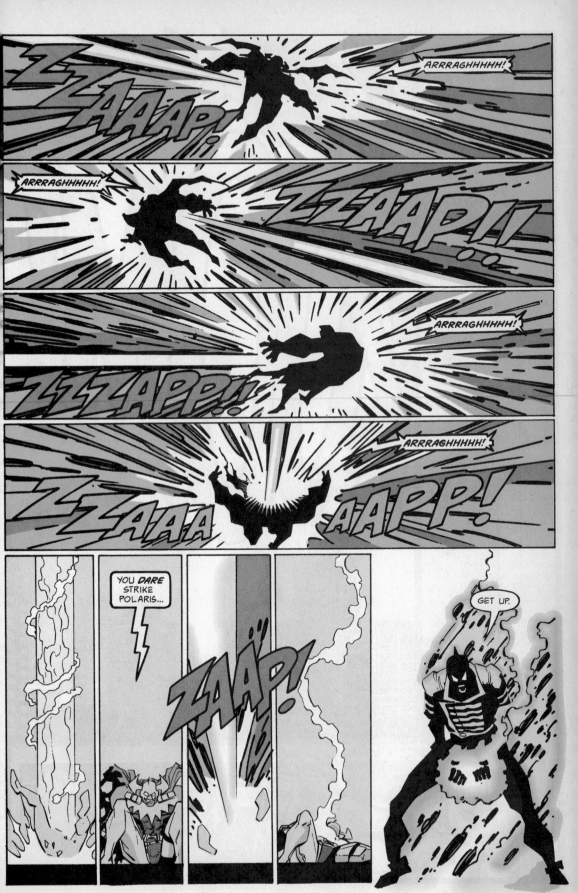

137

COVER GALLERY